Bunny School

CLOVER

Bunny School

By Ida DeLage

Drawings by Tracy McVay

GARRARD PUBLISHING COMPANY
CHAMPAIGN, ILLINOIS

Bunny School

Little bunnies!
Come in.
It is time to go
to school.

Look at your ears!
Look at your paws!

Wash!
Wash your ears.
Wash your paws.
You must be clean
for school.

Good-bye, little bunnies.
Go to school.
Be good.

Good-bye, Mother Bunny.
We will be good.
Good-bye.

Good morning, little bunnies.

Good morning, teacher.

Now it is time
for school.
Look! Look!
Listen! Listen!

Look!
This is clover.
Clover is good to eat.
Bunnies can eat
good clover.

Listen!
A bee goes
bzz-bzz.
Eat the good clover.
But . . .
do not eat a bee.

Look!
This is a fox.
He is red.
He has a big tail.

If you see a fox,
go thump, thump, thump.
You run, run, run
and jump, jump, jump.

Look!

This is a farmer.

FARMER

If you see the farmer,
go thump, thump, thump.
You run, run, run
and jump, jump, jump.

FARMER

Oh, oh!
Boopy Bunny
is not good.

Boopy was bad.
Now he is sad.

Come, little bunnies.
Hop along.
Hop, hop, hop.
We shall look for
some good clover.

Listen!

I hear bzz-bzz.

I hear some bees.

Look!

I see some clover.

Oh, oh!
We see something.
It is red.
It has a big tail.
The fox! The fox!

Go thump, thump, thump

Run, run, run

and jump, jump, jump.

No, no, little bunnies.

It is not the fox.

It is the cow.

A cow is good.

Come back.

Come back, little bunnies.

Eat.

Eat the clover.

We can eat

the good, good clover.

The farmer!
We see the farmer.
Go thump, thump, thump.
Run, run, run
and jump, jump, jump.

No, no, little bunnies.
It is not the farmer.
It is just the scarecrow.
Come back!
Come back!

Look out!
Look out, Boopy!
See the bee.
Do not eat the bee.

Oh, oh!
Poor Boopy!
You did not see
the bee.

Come, little bunnies.
It is time to go.
Hop along.
Hop, hop, hop.

Good-bye, little bunnies.

Good-bye, teacher.

Mother Bunny!
We did not see the fox.
We did not see the farmer.
Look!
We have some good clover
for you.